Only just then, a mistake happened.

'Cause I didn't even know there was a rip in my plumpery pillow. And so the next time I hit Grace, all of my feathers exploded out of it!

There was a million bazillion of those floaty things.

They filled the whole air, practically.

Lucille did a gasp.

That Grace did a gasp, too.

I danced around very giggling.

"HEY! IT'S SNOWING!" I said. "IT'S SNOWING! IT'S SNO—"

Just then, the door swinged opened very fast!

It was Lucille's nanna!

The Junie B. Jones series by Barbara Park

Junie B. Jones and the Stupid Smelly Bus #1
Junie B. Jones and a Little Monkey Business #2
Junie B. Jones and Her Big Fat Mouth #3
Junie B. Jones and Some Sneaky Peeky Spying #4
Junie B. Jones and the Yucky Blucky Fruitcake #5
Junie B. Jones and That Meanie Jim's Birthday #6
Junie B. Jones Loves Handsome Warren #7
Junie B. Jones Has a Monster Under Her Bed #8
Junie B. Jones Is Not a Crook #9
Junie B. Jones Is a Party Animal #10

Books for middle-grade readers by Barbara Park

Don't Make Me Smile
Operation: Dump the Chump
Skinnybones
Beanpole
The Kid in the Red Jacket
Almost Starring Skinnybones
My Mother Got Married (And Other Disasters)
Maxie, Rosie, and Earl—Partners in Grime
Rosie Swanson: Fourth-Grade Geek for President
Dear God, Help!!! Love, Earl
Mick Harte Was Here

Junie B. Jones
Is a
Party Animal

by Barbara Park
illustrated by Denise Brunkus

A STEPPING STONE BOOK™

Random House 🏠 New York

Text copyright © 1997 by Barbara Park
Illustrations copyright © 1997 by Denise Brunkus

http://www.randomhouse.com/

Library of Congress Cataloging-in-Publication Data
Park, Barbara. Junie B. Jones is a party animal / by Barbara Park ;
illustrated by Denise Brunkus.
    p. cm.
"A Stepping Stone book."
SUMMARY: Lucille invites Junie B. and her friend Grace to sleep over
at her very rich nanna's house, where everything is beautiful,
expensive, and breakable.
ISBN 0-679-88663-X (pbk.) — ISBN 0-679-98663-4 (lib. bdg.)
[1. Grandmothers—Fiction.   2. Wealth—Fiction.]
I. Brunkus, Denise, ill.   II. Title.
PZ7.P2197Jtwj   1997   [Fic]—dc21   97-17320

Printed in the United States of America 10 9 8 7 6 5 4 3 2
A STEPPING STONE BOOK is a trademark of Random House, Inc.

Contents

1. The Richiest Nanna   1
2. Excellent Work of Us   8
3. The Rules   16
4. Packing My Bags   22
5. Going to the Ball   31
6. Bouncing   44
7. Peeping   61
8. Morning   64

1/ The Richiest Nanna

My name is Junie B. Jones. The B stands for Beatrice. Except I don't like Beatrice. I just like B and that's all.

I am almost six years old.

Almost six is when you ride the bus to afternoon kindergarten.

My bestest friend named Grace rides the bus with me.

Every day she sits right exactly next to me. 'Cause I save her a seat, that's why.

Saving a seat is when you zoom on the bus. And you hurry up and sit down. And then you quick put your feet on the seat next to you.

After that, you keep on screaming the word "SAVED! SAVED! SAVED!" And no one even sits next to you. 'Cause who wants to sit next to a screamer? That's what I would like to know.

Me and that Grace have another bestest friend at school. Her name is Lucille.

Lucille does not ride the bus with us. Her richie nanna drives her to school in a big gold car. It is called a Cattle Act, I think.

And guess what?

Today that big gold Cattle Act was driving right next to the school bus!

I banged on my window very excited.

"LUCILLE! HEY, LUCILLE! IT'S ME! IT'S JUNIE B. JONES! I AM RIGHT NEXT TO YOU ON THE SCHOOL BUS!

SEE ME? SEE ME, LUCILLE? I AM BANGING ON MY WINDOW VERY EXCITED!"

Lucille did not see me.

"YEAH, ONLY HERE'S THE PROB-LEM! YOUR NANNA JUST SPEEDED UP HER CAR. AND NOW YOU ARE ZOOMING WAY AHEAD OF THE BUS. AND SO HOW COME I AM STILL SHOUTING AT YOU? THAT'S WHAT I WOULD LIKE TO KNOW."

I sat down and smoothed my skirt.

"Lucille's nanna has a lead foot, appar-ently," I said to that Grace.

"Lucille's nanna is rich," she said back.

"Lucille's nanna is very, *very* rich," I said. "She owns a big, giant house with a million rooms in it. And she lets Lucille's whole entire family live there. 'Cause it is way too big for just one nanna."

"Wow," said that Grace.

"I know it is wow, Grace," I said. "My nanna just owns a plain, old, regular house, and that's it."

That Grace did a sad sigh.

"My nanna just owns a condo in Florida," she said.

Then me and that Grace looked at each other very glum.

"Our nannas are losers," I said.

After that, we didn't talk the rest of the trip.

Only guess what?

When we got to school, we saw the nanna's big gold car! It was parked right in the parking lot!

Me and that Grace runned there speedy fast.

"Lucille! Lucille! It's me! It's Junie B. Jones! Plus also it's that Grace! We are running to see your richie nanna!"

We opened the door and sticked our heads inside.

"Hi, Nanna!" I said.

"Hello, Nanna!" said that Grace.

The nanna looked surprised at us.

"Yeah, only you don't even have to be afraid of us," I said. "'Cause we know your grandgirl very good. Plus we won't even harm you."

Me and that Grace got in the back.

I rubbed my hand on the seat.

"Oooo! I love this rich velvety interior," I told her.

I put my cheek on it.

"These seats are ooo-la-la, Nanna," I said.

Lucille looked grouchy at me. "Don't call
her *nanna!* She's *my* nanna! Not *your*
nanna!"

"Lucille!" said the nanna very shocked.
"What's gotten into you? Your little friends
are darling."

"Yes, Lucille," I said. "I am darling. Plus
that Grace is darling. And so, back off.
Right, Nanna?"

The nanna did a loud hoot of laughing.

"Hey! You are the friendliest nanna I ever saw!" I said. "And so maybe me and Grace can come see your richie house sometime."

Lucille's nanna did another loud hoot.

Then me and that Grace did loud hoots, too. And all of us kept on laughing and laughing.

Only not Lucille.

2/ Excellent Work of Us

Lucille sits at my same table in Room Nine.

She kept on being mad at me. Only I don't even know why.

"That is a lovely sweater you are wearing today, Lucille," I said very pleasant.

She scooted her chair away from me.

I scooted next to her.

"Oooo. Is that sequins I see on the collar? 'Cause sequins are my favorite little, shiny, roundish beady things," I told her.

I touched one of the sequins.

Lucille pushed my hand away.

I tickled her under the chin very friendly.

"Coochie-coochie-coo," I said real fun.

Lucille turned her back to me.

I swinged her ponytail.

"Swingy, swingy, swingy," I sang.

Just then, Lucille springed out of her chair.

"STOP TOUCHING ME!" she hollered right in my face.

My teacher hurried to my table speedy fast.

Her name is Mrs.

She has another name, too. But I just like Mrs. and that's all.

I smiled at her very cute.

"Hello. How are you today? Me and Lucille are not even fighting. We are just having a loudish conservation."

Mrs. looked funny at me.

"I think you mean *conversation*, Junie B.," she said. "*Conservation* is when people save something."

I tapped on my chin very thinking.

Then all of a sudden, I jumped up real excited.

"Yeah, only I *do*, Mrs.! I *do* save something!" I said. "I save that Grace a seat on the bus!"

I shouted across the room. "GRACE! HEY, GRACE! TELL MRS. HOW I SAVE YOU A SEAT ON THE BUS! 'CAUSE SHE THINKS I DON'T KNOW MY WORDS, APPARENTLY!"

That Grace shouted back. "SHE DOES, TEACHER! JUNIE B. SAVES ME A SEAT ON THE BUS EVERY SINGLE DAY!"

I smiled very proud. "See, Mrs.? I told

you! I told you I save something!"

Mrs. stared at me a real long time.

Then she closed her eyes.

And she said she needs a vacation.

Pretty soon, the bell rang for recess.

Lucille didn't even wait for me and Grace. She runned right out the door without us.

That is how come we had to chase that girl down and surround her.

I made my voice very growly.

"I am at the end of my string with you, madam!" I said. "How come you keep being mad at us? 'Cause me and Grace didn't even do anything to you!"

Lucille stamped her foot.

"Yes, you did! You ruined everything! I was begging my nanna for a little white poodle! And she was almost going to say yes! And then you guys got in my back seat! And now everything is ruined!"

I did a huffy breath at her.

"Yeah, only that is not even our fault, Lucille! 'Cause we didn't know you were begging! We just wanted to see your richie nanna, and that's all!"

"I don't care!" said Lucille. "You should have stayed away! You guys have your *own* nannas!"

Just then, me and that Grace got very glum again.

"I *know* we have nannas, Lucille," I said. "But they are not *richie* nannas like yours."

That Grace hanged her head.

"Our nannas are just *regular* nannas," she said.

"They are duds," I said real soft.

After that, Lucille acted nicer to us.

"Sorry," she said. "Sorry about your regular nannas. I was just upset about not getting my poodle, that's all. Usually my nanna gives me whatever I want."

Just then, I smiled real big. 'Cause a great idea popped in my head, that's why! It came right out of thin hair!

"Lucille! Hey, Lucille! Maybe me and Grace can come to your nanna's house! And we can help you beg for a poodle!"

I danced all around.

"And here is *another* great idea! Maybe we can even spend the night, possibly! 'Cause me and Grace never even saw a richie house before! Plus that way we can beg for your poodle the whole entire evening!"

All of a sudden, that Grace started dancing all around, too. "When can we come? When can we come?" she asked.

I clapped my hands very thrilled.

"I am available on Saturday, I believe!" I said.

"Me, too! I am available on Saturday, too!" said that Grace.

Lucille thought and thought.

"Hmm. I don't know about Saturday," she said. "My mommy and daddy and brother are going away for the weekend. So it's just going to be my nanna and me."

I jumped up and down.

"Hurray!" I said. "That will work out even better! 'Cause now we can beg your nanna with positively no interruptions!"

Just then, Lucille started to smile.

"Hey, yeah! Why didn't *I* think of that?" she said.

I pointed at myself.

"'Cause I'm the brains of this outfit, that's why!" I said real happy.

After that, all of us skipped around and around.

Plus me and that Grace did a high five.

'CAUSE WE WERE ON OUR WAY TO THE NANNA'S, OF COURSE!!!

3/ The Rules

Guess what!!?! Guess what!!?!

On Friday, Lucille's nanna called my mother!

And she invited me to spend the night with Lucille on Saturday!

And Mother didn't even say no!

My feet zoomed all around the house when I heard that!

"I'M SPENDIN' THE NIGHT! I'M SPENDIN' THE NIGHT! I'M SPENDIN' THE NIGHT!" I shouted.

I zoomed into my baby brother Ollie's room.

"HEY, OLLIE! I'M SPENDIN' THE NIGHT! I'M SPENDIN' THE NIGHT! I'M SPENDIN' THE—"

Just then, Mother runned in the door and she swished me right out of there.

It was not pleasant.

I brushed myself off.

"Yeah, only you shouldn't actually swish people," I said kind of quiet.

Mother raised her voice at me.

"How many times, Junie B.? How many times have I told you to stay out of Ollie's room while he's sleeping? Huh? How many?"

I thinked for a minute.

"A million bazillion," I said. "But that is just a ballpark figure."

17

Mother glared at me very mad.

I rocked back and forth on my feet.

"A ballpark figure is when you don't know the actual figure. And so you make up a figure. 'Cause that will get people off your back," I explained. "My boyfriend named Ricardo told me that. His father sells insurance, I believe."

Mother tapped her angry foot.

"We are *not* talking about Ricardo's father, Junie B. We are talking about going into Ollie's room while he's sleeping. And besides, I haven't said that you could spend the night at Lucille's. I want to talk it over with your father first."

I hugged her leg.

"Please, Mother? Please? Please? I'll be good. I promise, I promise, I—"

Just then, the front door opened.

It was my Daddy!

He was home from work!

I runned to him like a speedy rocket.

Then I hugged his leg, too. And he couldn't even shake me off.

"I'll be good, Daddy! I promise! I promise! I promise!"

All of a sudden, Mother swished me away again. She put me down in the living room.

Then she and Daddy did whispering in the hall.

And guess what?

They said I could go to Lucille's!!!

"YIPPEE! YIPPEE! YIPPEE!" I shouted.

After that, I started to zoom some more. But Daddy quick grabbed me by my belt.

"Yeah, only here's the problem. I'm not actually zooming," I told him.

"No...*here's* the problem," said Daddy. "Before you spend the night with Lucille, you have to agree to the rules."

I raised up my eyebrows.

"Rules?" I asked. "There's rules involved?"

"*Lots* of rules," said Daddy.

Then he and Mother bended down next to me. And they told me the rules of spending the night.

They are: No *running, no jumping, no shouting, no squealing, no hollering, no snooping, no spying, no arguing, no fighting, no cheating at games, no talking back to the nanna, no breaking other people's toys, no grumping, no crying, no fibbing, no tickling people when they say no, no staying up late, and absolutely no head-butting.*

After I heard the rules, I did a sigh.

"Yeah, only that doesn't actually leave me much to work with," I said.

Mother ruffled my hair.

"Sorry, kiddo. But that's the deal," she said. "Take it or leave it."

"Take it!" I shouted out. "I'll take the deal!"

Then I kissed Mother and Daddy on their cheeks.

And I hugged them very tight.

And they couldn't shake me off again.

4 / Packing My Bags

The next morning was Saturday.

I jumped out of bed and runned to the kitchen.

Then I got a big, giant plastic bag. And I runned back to my room to pack for Lucille's.

First, I packed my favorite pillow. Then I packed my pajamas and my bathrobe and my slippers that look like bunnies. Also, I packed my blanket and my sheets and a small, attractive throw rug.

Finally, I packed my stuffed elephant named Philip Johnny Bob.

He looked up at me from inside the bag. *Yeah, only here's the problem,* he said. *You're not actually supposed to put me in a plastic bag. 'Cause I could suffercate in this thing.*

My eyes got big and wide.

"Oh no!" I said real upset. "I forgot about that!"

That's how come I quick got my scissors and cut air holes for that guy.

Philip Johnny Bob sniffed the air. *Better,* he said.

I petted his trunk. Then I went into the family room. And I watched cartoons till Mother got up.

Pretty soon, I heard her slippers in the hall.

"MOTHER! MOTHER! I'M ALL
READY!" I said. "I'M ALL READY TO
GO TO LUCILLE'S!"

I pulled Mother into my room and
showed her my plastic bag.

Mother shook her head. "Waaaay too much stuff," she said.

Then she got a teeny suitcase from the shelf. And she packed my pajamas and my slippers and my robe and my toothbrush.

After that, she got a sleeping bag from her closet. And she put my pillow on top of it.

"There. That's all you'll need. You're all set," she said.

I springed into the air.

"ALL SET!" I hollered real joyful. "JUNIE B. JONES IS ALL SET FOR LUCILLE'S!"

After that, I quick grabbed Philip Johnny Bob. And I dragged my stuff to the front door.

"ALL RIGHTIE! LET'S BE ON OUR WAY!" I shouted very excited.

Mother was in baby Ollie's room. She didn't come.

"OKIE DOKE! I'M GOING OUTSIDE NOW! JUNIE B. JONES IS GOING OUTSIDE TO GET IN THE CAR!" I shouted louder.

Just then, Mother runned to get me.

"No, Junie B.! No! I'm not taking you to Lucille's, remember? Lucille's nanna is picking you up at three o'clock. I told you that. I'm *sure* I did."

All of a sudden, my shoulders got very slumping. 'Cause I didn't actually remember that information, that's why.

"Darn it," I said very sad. "Three o'clock takes forever."

After that, I slumped to the table and ate my breakfast.

Then I sat on my front step.

And I swinged on my swings.

And I read some books.

And I ate a cheese sandwich.

And I counted to a million bazillion.

And I sat on my step some more.

And then guess what?

Three o'clock finally came!

I saw the big gold car in my driveway!

"HEY! SHE'S HERE! SHE'S HERE! SHE'S HERE!" I yelled real thrilled.

Mother and Daddy hurried to the door.

"Are you ready to go?" said Mother.

"READY!" I yelled. "JUNIE B. JONES IS READY TO GO!"

The richie nanna got out of her car.

I throwed my arms around her.

"HELLO, NANNA! HELLO! HELLO! I HAVE BEEN WAITING FOR YOU THE WHOLE LIVELONG DAY!"

Mother pulled me off of that woman.

"Sorry," she said. "I'm afraid Junie B. has a little extra energy in her. She's been sitting on the step for hours."

I leaped way high in the air.

"SITTING ON THE STEP!" I said. "JUNIE B. JONES HAS BEEN SITTING ON THE STEP!"

Daddy and Mother carried my things to the big gold Cattle Act.

And guess what? When they opened the door, Lucille and that Grace were already in the backseat!

"LUCILLE! GRACE! I DIDN'T EVEN KNOW YOU WERE ALREADY HERE! AND SO THIS IS A DELIGHTFUL SURPRISE!"

I reached inside to try to tickle them. But Mother pulled my hand away.

"Please, Junie B. Don't start," she said.

I saluted her.

"Aye, aye, Captain," I said real hilarious.

After that, I got in the car and I bounced on the softie seat.

Only too bad for me. 'Cause I accidentally bounced too high. And I banged my head on the roof.

The nanna did a gasp.

I patted her.

"Yeah, only that didn't even faze me," I said.

After that, I buckled up my seat belt.

And I waved good-bye to Mother and Daddy.

And the nanna drove us away.

5/ Going to the Ball

Lucille was sitting in the middle.

She whispered real quiet to me and that Grace.

"Beg for my poodle," she said. "You *promised*, remember? You promised to beg for my poodle."

Me and that Grace looked and looked at each other. 'Cause we didn't actually want to do that particular thing.

Lucille poked us.

"Come on! You *promised!*" she whispered. "You promised to beg!"

I did a sigh.

Then I thinked and thinked about what to say.

Finally, I took a deep breath.

"Hey, Nanna. Guess what? Lucille wants a poodle, apparently. And so could you buy her one, do you think?" I asked.

"Yes, could you?" asked that Grace. "'Cause she is making us beg you. Or else we can't spend the night."

The nanna's mouth came all the way open.

"Ohhhh. So *that's* what this is all about, huh? Well, my granddaughter knows perfectly well that I am allergic to dogs. So you can tell Lucille that a poodle is out of the question, I'm afraid."

I patted Lucille very understanding.

"A poodle is out of the question, we're afraid," I said.

Lucille kicked her feet up and down.

"Beg *harder,*" she whispered. "You have to beg *harder.*"

I did a frown.

"Are you firm on that, Nanna?" I asked.

"No poodle, Lucille!" said the nanna very snappish.

Lucille kicked her feet some more.

"I *knew* that dumb idea wouldn't work!" she grouched.

Just then, the car stopped in front of a big iron gate.

Grace's eyes opened big and wide.

"Wow! This gate looks like a *castle* gate," she said.

Lucille smiled a teeny bit.

"It's not a castle gate, you sillyhead,

33

Grace," she said. "This is the gate to my *house*."

The nanna pushed a button, and the gate opened right in front of our eyes.

"Hey, that button is like *magic!*" I said.

Lucille smiled bigger.

After that, the nanna drove down a long driveway. She stopped in front of a big, beautiful house.

Lucille jumped out of the car and ran inside.

Me and that Grace followed after her.

And guess what? Lucille's house was even beautifuller on the *inside* than it was on the *outside!*

There was a beautiful long row of stairs. And a beautiful big bowl of flowers. And a beautiful, giant, sparkly ceiling light made out of glass.

I did a gasp at that glistening thing!

"That light takes my breathing away!" I said.

Lucille skipped all around in a circle.

She singed a loud song in our ears.

"SEE? SEE? I TOLD YOU I WAS RICH! SEE? SEE? I TOLD YOU I WAS RICH!" she sang.

She made that song up, I believe.

After that, she took our hands and showed us all the rooms in her house.

She showed us the living room. And the dining room. And the kitchen. And the big giant patio. And the daddy's office. And the mother's office. And the family room. And the pool room where you play pool. And the outside pool where you swim. And the hot tub. And the library. And the gym. And the nanna's room. And the mother and daddy's room. And the fancy gold bathroom with the Jacuzzi. And the brother's room. And a whole, whole bunch of guest rooms.

Then finally, Lucille showed us her very own bedroom!

And it looked like a bedroom where a princess lived!

Lucille's bed had a pink frilly roof on top of it.

"That is called a *canopy*," she explained. "It matches my pink silk draperies and my pink silk bedspread. And my pink telephone. And my plush pink rug. And my wallpaper with pink flowers in it.

"And see my TV? And my stereo? And my computer? And my CD player?"

She pointed to the corner. "And did you notice all of my big stuffed animals standing over there?" she asked.

My eyes popped out at those giant guys. The giraffe was bigger than me even!

Me and that Grace ran to play with them.

"NO! STOP! DON'T!" shouted Lucille. "YOU'RE NOT ALLOWED TO TOUCH THEM! THEY ARE JUST FOR SHOW!"

"Huh?" said that Grace.

"What?" I said. "How come?"

"Because they were expensive, *that's* how come," she said. "Those animals costed my nanna a fortune."

"Oh," I said kind of disappointed.

"Oh," said that Grace.

We sat down on Lucille's bed.

Lucille shouted at us again. "NO! GET UP! YOU'RE NOT ALLOWED TO SIT THERE! THAT BEDSPREAD IS JUST FOR SHOW!"

Me and that Grace springed right off of there.

Lucille quick smoothed the material with her hand.

"Don't you two know *anything?*" she said. "This bedspread is made out of *silk*, I told you. I'm not allowed to get it soiled."

"Oh," I said.

"Oh," said that Grace.

After that, Lucille skipped over to her dresser. And she pressed a button on her mirror.

A million bazillion lights came on!

"Look at this," she said. "This is my very own professional makeup mirror! It is the same kind of mirror that they use for movie stars. My nanna brought it all the way from Hollywood, California!"

Me and that Grace runned to the sparkly

mirror. We looked at ourselves in the bright
lights.

Then we sticked out our tongues and
made funny faces.

Lucille quick turned it off.

"It is *not* a toy!" she grouched.

After that, me and that Grace just stood

very still. And we didn't touch anything.

"This is going to be a long evening," I said kind of quiet.

Only just then, something very wonderful happened!

Lucille's nanna came in the room! And she was carrying a big box of dress-up clothes!

"I thought you little gals might have fun with some of my old evening gowns," she said real nice. "They're as old as the hills. But they're still quite stunning."

Lucille runned to the box speedy quick.

"Let's play Cinderella!" she said.

She pulled out a beautiful, sparkly pink gown.

"I'M CINDERELLA!" she shouted.

Then that Grace shoved me out of her way. And she runned to the box, too.

She pulled out a sparkly *blue* gown.

"I'M THE FAIRY GODMOTHER!" she yelled.

I did a huffy breath at those two. 'Cause now I had to be the ugly stepsisters, probably.

I bended down and searched through the box very careful.

Then all of a sudden, my hands felt something long and silky and softie.

I quick pulled it out of there.

The nanna's whole face lighted up.

"Oh my goodness! My old feather boa!" she said. "Why, I haven't seen that thing in years!"

I danced all around with that lovely thing.

"I love this, Nanna! I love this old feather boa!"

Just then, another great idea popped in my brain.

"Hey! I know! I will be the famous singer that sings at Cinderella's ball!"

Lucille and Grace looked funny at me.

"What singer?" said Lucille.

"There's no singer," said that Grace.

I stamped my foot at them.

"Yes, there is! There is, too, a singer! And I am her! And my name is Florence the Famous Singer! And I will be performing

show tunes from the hit musical *Annie!* So there!"

Lucille and Grace shrugged their shoulders at me.

Then they dressed up in their beautiful gowns.

And they went to the ball.

And I sang "The Sun Will Come Out Tomorrow."

6/Bouncing

After we finished playing Cinderella, the nanna called us to dinner.

Me and Lucille and that Grace skipped into the big dining room. We sat at a long, shiny table.

Pretty soon, Lucille's nanna came in from the kitchen. And she gave us our dinner.

And guess what?

Its name was beans and Frank!

"Hurray!" I said. "Hurray for beans and

Frank! 'Cause this is my favorite kind of home cooking!"

The nanna did a teeny smile.

"Well, we usually have a cook. But I gave her the night off," she said.

After that, the nanna poured milk into beautiful sparkly glasses.

"Oooo, Nanna! These are your best crystal glasses!" said Lucille real thrilled. "I love these expensive things!"

"Me, too! I love these expensive things, too!" I said.

Only too bad for me. 'Cause nobody even told me that crystal glasses were very heavy.

And so when I picked up my glass, it slipped right out of my hand.

And it fell on the floor!

And it broke into lots of pieces!

Lucille's whole mouth came open.

"OH NO! YOU BROKE IT! YOU BROKE MY NANNA'S CRYSTAL GLASS!"

The nanna's face was reddish and scrunchy.

"Sorry, Nanna," I said real soft. "Sorry I broke your crystal glass."

The nanna sucked her cheeks way into her head.

"Let's just try to be more careful, shall we, dear?" she said.

I bobbed my head up and down.

"We shall," I said back.

After that, I ate my beans and Frank very careful. Only pretty soon, my Frank spilled off my fork. And he landed on the nanna's white tablecloth.

"OH NO!" hollered Lucille. "THAT'S MY NANNA'S GOOD LINEN TABLE-

CLOTH! SHE BROUGHT IT ALL THE WAY FROM IRELAND!"

The nanna's face was twisty and puffy.

I quick pushed my plate away from me.

My stomach felt in a tight knot.

"Yeah, only guess what? I am not actually hungry anymore. And so I will just sit here and not spill anything, I think."

The nanna cleaned up my messes with a wet cloth.

After she finished, she brought us chocolate ice cream for dessert.

Only too bad for me. 'Cause a teeny plop of ice cream dropped right off my spoon. And it landed on my chair cushion.

The nanna did a big breath.

"You're a bit of a bull in a china shop, aren't you, dear?" she said.

"Sorry, Nanna," I said. "Sorry, sorry, sorry."

The nanna patted my hand very stiffish.

"Quite all right," she said kind of mumbly.

After that, I got down from the table. And me and my friends went back to Lucille's room.

And guess what?

Things got funner!

'Cause Lucille said we could play with the games in her closet! On account of they weren't even expensive!

First, we played Chutes and Ladders. Then we played Twister and Bingo and Chinese checkers and Tic-Tac-Toad and Candyland. Plus also we played Let's Spin Till We Get Real Dizzy and Fall Down.

And guess what? I didn't even break any-thing!

"Hey! I think I am getting the hang of this party!" I said very happy.

Just then, the nanna knocked on Lucille's door.

"Time for you ladies to put your pajamas on," she told us.

I danced all around the room real happy.

"Hurray!" I said "Hurray for pajamas! 'Cause I brought my favorites!"

I quick put them on.

"See them, Nanna? See how biggish and baggish they are? That is how come they feel so comfortable!"

The nanna's eyes looked down at me.

"How very...*charming*," she said.

Just then, that Grace jumped right in front of me.

"Look at mine, Nanna!" she said. "See

49

mine? My pajamas have neon-green polka dotties on them!"

"How very…*colorful*," said the nanna.

All of a sudden, Lucille popped out of her big closet.

"Ta-da! Look at *me*, everyone! I am wearing my beauteous pink satin nightie! See me? See how lovely I look! I look like a gorgeous model in this thing!" she said.

Lucille let me and that Grace feel her material.

"How very…*smoothie*," I said.

After that, me and Grace unrolled our sleeping bags on the floor. And the nanna took the silk bedspread off Lucille's bed.

"Time to get your beauty sleep, Princess," she told Lucille.

Then those two kissed and hugged good night. And the nanna shut the door.

Only guess what?

Lucille didn't even get in bed. She kept twirling all around in her pink satin night-gown.

"This is how models twirl," she said. "They twirl so you can see their fronts and their backs."

Lucille wouldn't stop twirling.

"See my front? See my back?" she said.

Me and that Grace got up on her bed to watch her twirl.

Lucille's bed was soft and cushy.

We bounced up there a teeny bit.

Lucille stopped twirling.

"Hey! Don't!" she said. "That bed is for beauty sleep *only!*"

I patted her bed very admiring.

"Yeah, only it's too bad we can't actually play up here. 'Cause this mattress is a *bouncy* one," I said.

Just then, Lucille's face did a sneaky smile.

"Want to bounce?" she said real soft.

"Want to really, *really* bounce?"

She tippytoed to her door and looked down the hall.

"Come on," she whispered. "Follow me."

I grabbed Philip Johnny Bob and followed after Lucille and that Grace.

We tippytoed down the hall and around the corner.

Then Lucille opened the door to a big guest room. And there was a giant bed in that place!

"See it!" she said. "See how *huge* that bed is? My nanna had it specially made in case we have tall company!"

Lucille quick shut the door after us.

"Come on! Let's go!" she said.

And so all of us runned to the big bed speedy quick! And we jumped and jumped and jumped on that thing!

I sang a joyful song.

It is called "Jumping, Jumping, Jumping on the Giant Bed."

"JUMPING...JUMPING...JUMPING ON THE GIANT BED," I sang.

Only too bad for me. 'Cause all of a sudden, I remembered something very important. And it is called *Mother and Daddy said no jumping*.

I got off the bed speedy fast.

"Yeah, only here's the problem," I said. "I am not actually allowed to jump. 'Cause Mother and Daddy said *no jumping*. And so you guys should stop jumping, too. 'Cause that would be polite of you."

Lucille and that Grace didn't pay attention to me.

That is how come I had to get back on the giant bed and shout in their faces.

"STOP JUMPING, I SAID! 'CAUSE I AM NOT ALLOWED TO JUMP! AND YOU GUYS SHOULDN'T JUMP, TOO!"

Grace springed way high in the air.

"Who's jumping? I'm not jumping," she said.

She giggled very silly. "I'm *bouncing!*"

Just then, my whole face got happy.

I hugged and hugged that girl.

'Cause Mother and Daddy didn't say I couldn't *bounce!*

After that, I bounced and bounced and bounced.

"BOUNCING...BOUNCING...BOUNCING ON THE GIANT BED," I sang.

I bounced till sweat came on my head.

Then I flopped down on the bed to rest.

I flopped on a plumpery pillow.

"Oooo, Lucille! This is the most

plumpery pillow I ever even saw!" I told her.

"Of *course* it is, silly," said Lucille. "That's because my nanna has all her pillows handmade in Sweden."

I quick swinged the plumpery pillow over to my friend Grace.

"Grace! Hey, Grace! Feel how plumpery this pillow is!" I said.

Only Grace didn't actually see it coming. And it accidentally hit her in the head.

I peeked at her under that thing.

"Yeah, only that did not even harm you, I bet. 'Cause plumpery pillows don't hurt people. Right, Grace. Right?"

That Grace did a teeny grin.

Then she took the plumpery pillow off her head. And she swinged it all around. And she hit me in the tummy!

"Ooomph!" I said.

Then I laughed and laughed.

"Hey! I was right! Plumpery pillows *don't* hurt people!"

After that, I hit Lucille in the head with my plumpery pillow. Plus also, I hit Grace again.

Then those guys got their own plumpery pillows. And all of us kept on hitting each other very fun!

Only just then, a mistake happened. 'Cause I didn't even know there was a rip in my plumpery pillow. And so the next time I hit Grace, all of my feathers exploded out of it!

There was a million bazillion of those floaty things.

They filled the whole air, practically.

Lucille did a gasp.

That Grace did a gasp, too.

I danced around very giggling.

"HEY! IT'S SNOWING!" I said. "IT'S SNOWING! IT'S SNO—"

Just then, the door swinged opened very fast!

It was Lucille's nanna!

She saw me holding the broken plumpery pillow!

My heart pounded hard inside of me.

"Hello," I said very nervous. "How are

you today? I am fine. Except I am having a little bit of a feather problem, apparently."

The nanna walked at me very slow.

Then she took my pillow out of my hands.

And she hided her face in that flatty thing.

And she didn't come out for a real long time.

7/ Peeping

After a while, the nanna took us back to Lucille's room.

Me and Philip Johnny Bob got in our sleeping bag speedy fast.

Then that Grace got in her sleeping bag, too. And Lucille got into her softie bed.

"Not one more peep out of you girls," said the nanna very grouchy. "Do you hear me? Not one more *peep*."

She turned off the light and shut the door.

I stayed quiet a real long time. 'Cause I

was scared of that woman, that's why.

All of a sudden, I heard a teeny voice.

"Peep!" it said. "Peep, peep, peep!"

It was Lucille.

Me and that Grace giggled out loud at her.

"Peep," said that Grace.

"Peep," I said.

Peep, said Philip Johnny Bob.

Then pretty soon, all of us were peeping all over the place.

"Peep, peep, peep, *peep*. Peep, peep, peep, *peep*."

Lucille kept on peeping louder and louder and louder.

"PEEP! PEEP! PEEP!" she said.

Also, she was giggling very hard.

Finally, me and that Grace sat up in our sleeping bags. We stared at that girl.

"Lucille is peeping out of control," said that Grace.

"Maybe she is overly tired," I said. "Overly tired makes your brain go silly."

"PEEP!" said Lucille. "PEEP! PEEP! PEEP! PEEP! PEEP!"

Just then, Lucille's nanna opened the door again.

"SILENCE!" she yelled real scary.

Shivers came on my skin.

Then all of us quick crawled under our covers again.

And we closed our eyes.

And we didn't say another peep.

8/Morning

Morning came very early.

It was still dark outside.

I jiggled Lucille and that Grace.

"I'm hungry," I said. "Are you guys hungry. I am really, *really* hungry."

I shook them some more.

"Let's eat. You wanna eat? I really, *really* wanna eat."

Finally, Lucille and that Grace yawned and stretched.

Then all of us put on our bathrobes and

our slippers. And we went down the hall to get the nanna for breakfast.

Lucille shaked her real gentle.

"Wake up, Nanna," she whispered.

"Wake up, Nanna," said that Grace.

"Wake up, Nanna," I said.

The nanna did a snore.

That's how come we had to pull her up by her arms. And we turned a bright light in her face.

The nanna yawned real big.

It was not pleasant.

After that, she got her robe and slippers. And she went downstairs with us.

We sat at the long dining room table again.

The nanna passed out cereal bowls.

"Oh, Nanna! These are the brand-new china bowls you bought in France!

These are my favorites!" said Lucille.

All of a sudden, I felt a knot in my stomach again.

I tapped on the nanna's hand.

"Yeah, only here's the problem. I think I would like to have a plastic cereal bowl.

'Cause plastic is more my style."

The nanna rolled her eyes way up at the ceiling. I looked up there, too. But I didn't see anything.

"I don't *own* any plastic cereal bowls," she said.

After that, she brought in the orange juice. And she poured it into teeny crystal glasses.

I got down from my chair.

"Yeah, only guess what? I think I will just stand here and not eat. Or else I might spill something again," I said.

The nanna looked and looked at me.

Then she went into the kitchen and she brought me back a banana.

"Here. Try this," she said kind of nicer.

I did a smile.

Then I ate my banana very careful.

And I didn't spill a drop.

Mother picked me up at nine o'clock.

She came into the nanna's big, beautiful house to get me.

"My! What a lovely home you have here," she said to the nanna.

Then Mother walked to the big bowl of beautiful flowers. And she tried to smell those lovely things.

"NO! DON'T! THEY ARE JUST FOR SHOW PROBABLY!" I hollered.

After that, I said good-bye to my friends. And I thanked the nanna. And I quick pulled Mother out of that house. Or else she might break something, that's why.

I runned down the steps and got in my car. Then I rubbed my hand on the backseat.

It was not as soft as the nanna's backseat.

I smiled very relieved.

"It's good to be back," I said.

Mother drove down the long driveway.

My stomach growled real loud.

"Guess what? My tummy is still hungry for breakfast. 'Cause I didn't actually eat much this morning," I said.

Mother laughed.

"I swear, Junie B. Your stomach is a bottomless pit," she said.

Just then, another great idea popped into my head!

"Mother! Hey, Mother! Maybe you and me can stop at Grandma Miller's for breakfast! 'Cause she fixes blueberry pancakes every Sunday morning! And blueberry pancakes is my favorite breakfast in the whole entire world!"

Mother thinked about my offer.

Then all of a sudden, she turned around the car. And we drove to my grandma Miller's house. And we were just in time for blueberry pancakes!

We ate a million bazillion of those delicious things!

Plus also I drank orange juice out of a plastic glass!

"Hurray!" I said. "Hurray for plastic!"

Then me and Grandma Miller hugged and hugged.

And guess what else?

I think I like my regular nanna just perfect.

Books are my Very **FAVORITE** things in the **Whole World!**

Read this next book about me. And **I mean it!**

*Junie B. Jones
Is a Beauty Shop Guy*

by **Barbara Park**

Coming in 1998

Barbara Park says:

66 When I was little, spending the night at a friend's house for the first time always felt like an adventure. I felt like a spy, almost. So many intriguing questions waiting to be answered.

What was her family like? What did they eat for dinner? Would I like it...or would I have to pretend to sneeze, and then quick spit it into my napkin? How late would I get to stay up? Were the parents nice...or would they yell at me if I got the giggles and couldn't go to sleep? What did everyone's pajamas look like? What did they have for breakfast? Were they rich? Whoa! That would be exciting, wouldn't it? To see how rich people lived?

When I put Junie B. into this position, I was almost as excited as she was. Finally, I'd get to spend the night in a rich person's house! (Even if it was only in my imagination.)

Needless to say, I was pretty surprised the way everything turned out. Even more surprised than Junie B., who ended up teaching me one of life's great lessons: *Rich is good...but blueberry pancakes are better.*

Who knew? **99**